AROUND OUR WAY ON NEIGHBORS' DAY

By TAMEKA FRYER BROWN   Illustrated by CHARLOTTE RILEY-WEBB

Abrams Books for Young Readers, New York

Blue sky, no clouds,
Summer heat, side street,
Whirling, whizzing feet.
Everyone is out to play
Today, around our way.

Blading, step dance, double Dutch.
Football game was way too much!
Shrika, Binh, and me—all sweating
In the blazing sun.

Look, here comes the ice-cream man!
Holding money in our hands,
We chase him down for frozen treats.
Quick! Lick before it runs.

Blue sky, no clouds.
Time to go.
I know
I'll see them later, so
I head home while they both stay
To play, around our way.

I peek in the barbershop.
Uncle Charlie and Grandpop
Are talking loud and arguing—
Debating with the men.

Run in quick to say "Hello"
And "Don't be late!" before I go
Strolling past the red oak tree.
I'm on my way again.

Blue sky, no clouds,
Corner store.
One more
Block to walk before
I'm home. It's a special day
Today, around our way.

Pass on sour lemonade
Those little Lindsay triplets made.
Wave to Raven working on her
Mural way up high.

Mr. O and Mr. Wong
Playing chess the whole day long.
Big kids at the center, hooping—
Flying through the sky.

Blue sky, no clouds.
Home to see
Daddy
Helping Mr. Lee.
This is known as Neighbors' Day
Today, around our way.

Sprinkling, stirring something hot
In the big, black iron pot.
Momma takes a taste, then she
Sprinkles it some more.

Ring! Ring! goes the telephone—
Momma leaves her pot alone.
Big mistake! "Oh no!" she screams,
And races 'cross the floor.

Blue sky, no clouds.
What to do?
Who knew
That we'd burn the food?
Cheese and noodles save the day
Today, around our way.

People come out to the street
With the food we love to eat:
Tante Elise's gumbo,
Mr. Junior's oxtail stew,

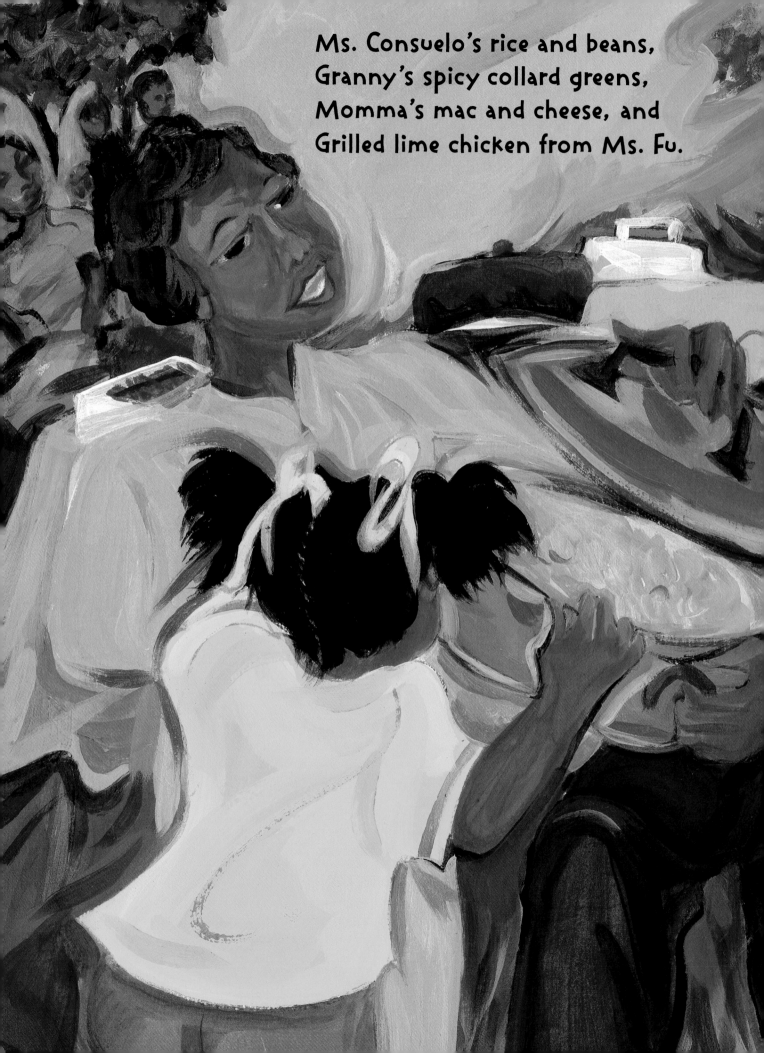

Ms. Consuelo's rice and beans,
Granny's spicy collard greens,
Momma's mac and cheese, and
Grilled lime chicken from Ms. Fu.

Blue sky, no clouds.
No one stares,
Or cares
That loud music blares.
Hustle . . . bustle . . . salsa sway,
Wild day, around our way.

Great big bubbles ride the breeze.
Trikes and bikes and skinned-up knees,
Dominoes, Bid Whist, and Spades—
No talking 'cross the board!

Down the double line, we dance.
Thumping rhythms—one more chance
To have my daddy's robot moves
Embarrass me some more.

Summer sunlight going down.
Smooth and easy, jazzy sound
Flowing from the saxophone that
Uncle Charlie plays.

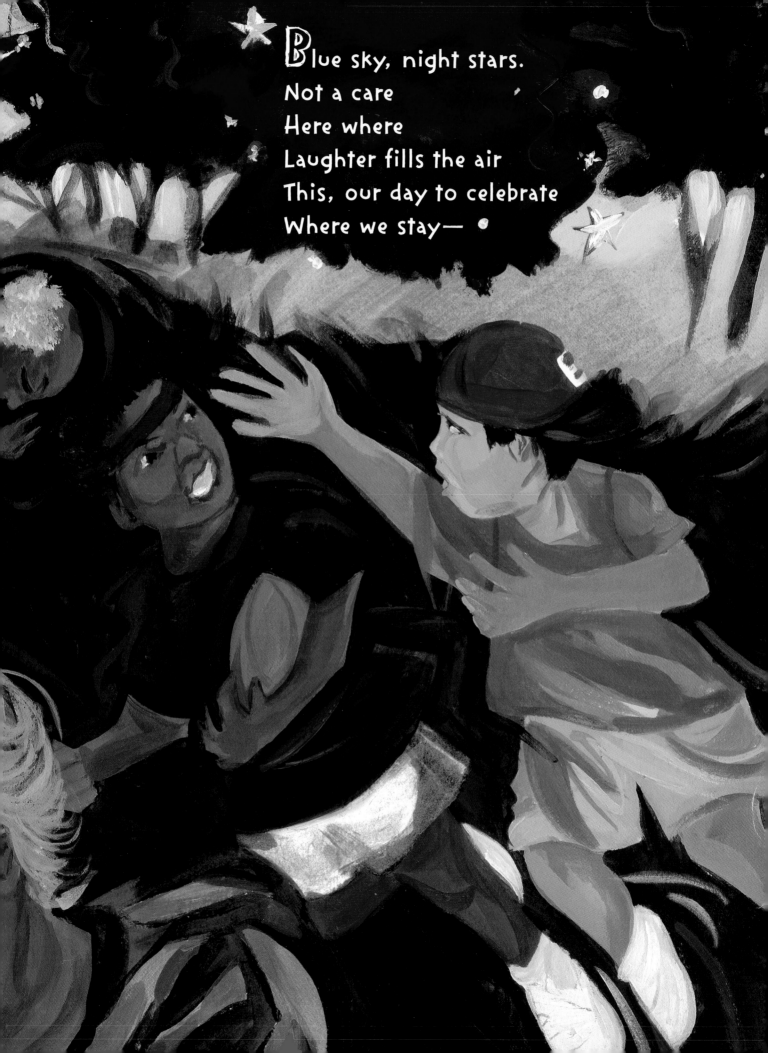

Blue sky, night stars.
Not a care
Here where
Laughter fills the air
This, our day to celebrate
Where we stay—

Today,

AROUND OUR WAY.

FOR AKHARI, KINAYA, AND DARAJA—IF I CAN, YOU CAN!
—T. F. B.

FOR MY FAMILY, EXTENDED FAMILY, AND ALL OF MY
DEAR FRIENDS. YOU ARE ALL SO SPECIAL IN MY LIFE.
—C. R.–W.

ARTIST'S NOTE

As I worked on *Around Our Way on Neighbors' Day*, I thought of the neighborhood camaraderie and block parties I experienced as a child and really enjoyed this unique opportunity to reminisce. My paint medium is acrylic.

AUTHOR'S ACKNOWLEDGMENTS

Thank you to all the family and friends who encourage me—especially my mother, Oscie; my husband, Niles; my aunt Ruby; my mom-in-law, Linda; and Adrien G.
Thank you to my daughters: Akhari (for your insight), Kinaya (for being my most passionate cheerleader), and Daraja (for liking Mommy's stories).
Thank you to Tamar Brazis and Jen Rofe for your excitement and your willingness.
Thank you to Kelly Starling-Lyons and Stephanie Greene for embracing and mentoring me from day one.
Thank you to my fellow Mudskippers for telling me what I need to hear, when I need to hear it. Mudskippers rock!
Most of all, thank you to my Father above . . . for blue skies without clouds, and for dreams that become realities.

Cataloging-in-Publication Data has been applied for and may be obtained from the Library of Congress.

ISBN 978-0-8109-8971-9

Printed and bound in China
10 9 8 7 6 5 4 3 2 1

Abrams Books for Young Readers are available at special discounts when purchased in quantity for premiums and promotions as well as fundraising or educational use. Special editions can also be created to specification. For details, contact specialmarkets@abramsbooks.com or the address below.

ABRAMS
THE ART OF BOOKS SINCE 1949
115 West 18th Street
New York, NY 10011
www.abramsbooks.com